e. 1

Chalmers, Mary
CHA
Six dogs, twenty-
three cats, forty-
five mice, and one
hundred sixteen
spiders

DATE			

*Six Dogs, Twenty-Three Cats, Forty-Five Mice,
and One Hundred Sixteen Spiders*

Six Dogs, Twenty-three Cats, Forty-five Mice, and One Hundred Sixteen Spiders
Copyright © 1986 by Mary Chalmers. Printed in the U.S.A. All rights reserved.

Library of Congress Cataloging-in-Publication Data
Chalmers, Mary, 1927–
   Six dogs, twenty-three cats, forty-five mice, and
one hundred sixteen spiders.

   Summary: Annie tries unsuccessfully to keep her
190 pets out of the company room to avoid frightening
her friend Priscilla.
   [1. Pets—Fiction.   2. Friendship—Fiction]   I. Title.
PZ7.C354Si 1986   [E]   83-49482
ISBN 0-06-021188-1
ISBN 0-06-021189-X (lib. bdg.)

Designed by Constance Fogler
1 2 3 4 5 6 7 8 9 10
First Edition

C. 1

Six Dogs,
Twenty-Three Cats,
Forty-Five Mice, and
One Hundred Sixteen Spiders

MARY CHALMERS

Harper & Row, Publishers
New York

Annie Tree lived in a little yellow house.

She had six dogs,

twenty-three cats,

forty-five mice,

and one hundred sixteen spiders living in her house.

Annie Tree knew the names of each and every one,
except for the two shy spiders
who lived in the teapot.

She just called them "Dears."
Every day she talked to them,
trying to coax them out.

And every day Annie Tree dusted and mopped and
scrubbed. But her house was never, ever, ever neat.

One day Priscilla Wicket came to visit.
"How nice to see you!" said Annie Tree.

They had tea with milk and a cake with layers
of raspberry jam and whipped cream.

"My, what a lot of dogs and cats you have!"
said Priscilla Wicket.

"Yes," said Annie Tree proudly.
"I have six dogs, twenty-three cats,
forty-five mice,
and one hundred sixteen spiders."

16

Just then, a little cat
decided to have a little lick of milk.
"Eeek!" cried Priscilla. "Excuse me,
I've got to run!"

And she did.

Annie Tree looked at the dogs under the table,
and the cats on top of the table.
She looked at the mice in the closet
and the spiders everywhere.
Then she called the carpenter.

"Make me a company room, please!" she told him.

When the room was finished,

Annie Tree invited Priscilla for tea and cake.
"What a lovely company room," exclaimed Priscilla.
"So tidy and neat!"
They drank freshly brewed tea
and nibbled on delicious chocolate cake.
It was so quiet.
No dogs. No cats. No mice. No spiders.

They were all on the other side of the door.

Annie Tree was beginning to think
how *very* quiet it was without her animals
when the two shy spiders
came looking for their teapot.
"Excuse me!" cried Priscilla. "I've got to run!"

And she did.

Annie Tree sighed.
She looked at the two shy spiders and smiled.
Then she opened the door and called,

"Come on in, everyone!
The Dears are already here!"

"Oh, my," sighed Annie Tree,
"I love each and every one of you.
But Priscilla is my friend, too.
She is not used to so many animals."
The six dogs, twenty-three cats, forty-five mice,
and one hundred sixteen spiders all felt sad
because Annie Tree was sad.

Just then there was a knock at the door.

It was Priscilla!

"I'm sorry I ran away," said Priscilla.

"You are my good friend, Annie.

I am just not used to so many animals all around me.

We can finish our tea now."

Annie Tree and Priscilla
had a happy visit in the company room.

The dogs did not jump.
The cats sat about quietly and licked their paws.
The mice and the spiders stayed out of sight.

Only the two shy spiders sat close by,
waiting for their teapot to be empty again.